The Dive

by Susan Delaney
illustrated by Michael Chesworth

 HOUGHTON MIFFLIN   BOSTON

Christy had waited all week for Megan's party at the public pool. And it was turning out to be lots of fun.

Christy showed everyone how to do a split jump.
She was just about to do a twist in the air. Then
Sara arrived.

Sara could dive. And everyone wanted to learn.

4

For the rest of the day, the pool was filled with the sound of the girls hitting the water on their bellies like little whales. By the end of the day, everyone had tried to dive. Everyone but Christy.

When she got home, Christy lay on her bed,
thinking about the party. "Diving is silly anyway,"
she thought. "Who wants to plop into the water
headfirst, like a frog?"

But she started doing pretend dives anyway. She puffed out her cheeks and swung her arms back. Just then, her brother walked in.

When he saw Christy, he began to laugh. "What are you, some kind of blowfish?" he asked.

KEEP OUT
this means
you,
NATHAN
!!!

Christy gave him a look that said, "Very funny." Then she asked, "Hey, Nathan, do you know how to dive?"

"Sure. Diving is easy," Nathan replied. He put his hands together and jumped onto Christy's bed. Then Nathan saw the hurt look on her face.

"I can help you," he said. Nathan showed her how to hold her arms and bend her legs.

Before dinner, Christy told her mom about the party. "Sara ruined it," she said. "She thinks she's so great because she knows how to dive."

Her mom gave her a funny look. "I thought you liked Sara," she said.

"I guess she's okay," Christy admitted. "But I don't like diving."

"Did you even try?" asked her mom.

"I can't!" Christy whined. "I hold my nose when I jump. You can't hold your nose and dive."

"You have to blow air out your nose," her mother said. She showed Christy what to do.

Christy thought her mom looked like a snorting dragon when she blew air out her nose. Christy decided to practice in front of a mirror before she tried it in public.

The next day, Christy, her mom, and Nathan headed for the town pool. When they got there, Sara was waiting for them.

"Hi, Christy," Sara said. "Want to practice diving together? Then maybe you can show me your split jump."

"Umm, okay," Christy said. She was still afraid.

"The first time I tried diving, I was really scared," said Sara, as if she could read Christy's mind. "But finally I closed my eyes and just dived right in. It was easy after that."

Then Christy's mom, and Nathan, and Sara all stood beside her at the edge of the pool. Suddenly, Christy didn't feel afraid!

Nathan raised his hands, and Christy raised
her hands. Christy's mother blew air out her nose,
and Christy blew air out her nose. Sara smiled.
She dived in. And Christy dived in right after her.